FIVE ON
BREXIT ISLAND

Enid Blyton®

FIVE ON
BREXIT ISLAND

Text by
Bruno Vincent

Enid Blyton for Grown-Ups

Quercus

First published in Great Britain in 2016 by

Quercus Editions Ltd
Carmelite House
50 Victoria Embankment
London EC4Y 0DZ

An Hachette UK company

A CIP catalogue record for this book is available
from the British Library

HB ISBN 978 1 78648 384 3
EBOOK ISBN 978 1 78648 385 0

Text by Bruno Vincent
Original illustrations by Eileen A. Soper
Cover illustration by Ruth Palmer

10 9 8 7 6 5 4 3 2 1

Typeset by CC Book Production

Printed and bound in Great Britain by Clays Ltd, St Ives plc

Contents

CHAPTER ONE

The Fate of Kirrin Island Hangs in the Balance

Julian cleared his throat and stepped forward.

'There's been a lot of scaremongering going on,' he said, 'about the potential consequences of this vote: about subsidies, about people's livelihoods being threatened, about the economy and about hope in the future. I wholeheartedly reject this rhetoric. It's disgraceful and it's cheap. And it's making this debate about something it shouldn't be: fear.'

He paused to allow this to sink in, and also to bask for a moment in how well the speech was going. The audience stirred in front of him. He consulted his notes, and went on.

'Fear is a dreadful thing. It makes us lose sight of what is really at stake, it blurs our vision. We must remember what made ours a great country. And we must fight to retain the *values* that make this country wonderful, that make it the place we have always loved. You see, I won't give those things up lightly! I shall fight for them, until I have no breath left to give!'

The audience rose to its feet.

'And if that makes me foolish, then I am glad to be a fool! Because I believe that Britain *is* great, and Kirrin Island is great too – and they are better . . . together!' He concluded his speech at the top of his voice, staring nobly into the distance.

The audience stretched and yawned, and after licking its paws, took notice of a passing butterfly, and trotted off to chase it.

'Oh, come on, Timmy,' said Julian. 'That was rousing stuff. Just you wait till some humans hear it! They'll be eating out of my hand! The only thing *you'll* eat out of my hand is sausages.'

'Woof!' said Timmy, bounding back towards him.

'Oh, typical electorate – you just want a bribe. I suppose you'll vote for me if I say "sausages"?'

'Woof, woof!' said Timmy, a love of democracy running through him like an electric current. 'Woof!'

'It's going to be a long campaign . . .' muttered Julian.

*'If there's one thing stronger than politics
it's friendship. Right?'*

Three days earlier ...

Waves were lapping quietly against the shore of Kirrin Island as the boat's prow nudged up against the pebbles. As always, the moment of landing on Kirrin Island made Julian, Anne, George and Dick let out a collective sigh of relief and satisfaction, while Timmy, barking loudly, leapt out of the boat and splashed ashore.

On this occasion, however, the weather was by no means welcoming. By the time they had tied up the boat and unpacked their luggage, it was obvious that the brooding sky was not going to hold its temper for much longer, and so they made straight for the ruins of Kirrin Castle – the only place on the island that offered protection from a storm.

They climbed up to the ruins and put their belongings in a heap not a moment too soon, because the rain started almost before they'd put the last bag down. Within seconds, it went from a few drops to an explosive deluge over which they had to shout to be heard.

'I could have been on the sofa now, eating leftover curry and watching *House of Cards*,' said Julian, hands on hips.

'And give up this enchanting possibility of death by pneumonia?' asked George, as the initial burst subsided somewhat and they could all hear each other again. 'I don't care about the weather; it's so good to be out of London while all those disgusting toffs are deciding our future, and droning on about who's going to be in charge.'

'I thought we agreed to keep politics out of this little holiday,' said Anne. 'We're escaping from all that.' As she spoke, Anne looked at Julian afresh. There seemed to be something different about him these days.

Formerly a svelte and smart man, Julian had lately been putting on a lot of weight – he was almost roly-poly. And perhaps because he hadn't adjusted his wardrobe, his clothes seemed no longer to fit – his shirts flapping free and a certain bulge appearing over his belt. What was more, although Julian had caught a lot of sun this summer, Anne wasn't sure that accounted for how blond he had got, nor for the way his hair flapped to and fro in such an ungainly fashion these days, when the wind caught it, and without him seeming to care a jot.

The overall impression left her rather unsettled, but instead of pursuing this train of thought, she quickly added, 'Besides, Julian, I'm sure this rain will clear up soon and we'll have a *lovely* time exploring.'

They all stood and looked at the downpour. They could

tell it wasn't the sort that blows itself out in a couple of minutes. It had settled into a steady and monotonous rhythm that seemed capable of continuing for hours.

'Let's make our home here, then,' Anne said. So she and Dick got on with setting up camp with pleasant determination, in order to distract the other two from disagreement. Holidaying on this island – much as they loved it dearly – always came with an inherent social tension, for Julian naturally thought of himself as the leader, and yet Kirrin Island belonged to George, lock, stock and barrel.

This tension had never led to an open argument or rift in the group, but that was partly owing to the vigilant diplomacy of Anne and Dick, which often (as now) took the form of cheerful distraction. The tents were up and a fire was laid in barely half an hour, and Anne took advantage of the fact that there were walls around them by prettifying the camp, hanging some attractive scarves and a lantern, and organizing the books and food people had brought into a miniature library and larder.

'The only thing this island could do with is some games for us to play,' Anne said thoughtfully.

'Julian would probably go for a whiff-whaff table,' George commented.

'Certainly not,' said Julian. 'In my house at Eton, we regarded "whiff-whaff" as a vulgar, modern term. We called it "pash-pish" – in fact a mistranslation from the original Aramaic,' he added loftily.

The fire lit, Timmy sat panting and drying himself after joyously chasing rabbits in the rain for the last hour, while George ventured out into the storm to get water from the well, for a pot of tea.

'I've even remembered the food, this time,' said Dick, opening a Tupperware box of prepared vegetables, and another of meat, and threading them on to kebab sticks. Watching him, Anne fanned the fire to see if it glowed hot enough.

The others chatted while Dick watched over the food. Perfect peace descended on the camp: a specific, personal sense of contentment, which these five always experienced when they were camping together. They were away from the city, far from civilization, and around a crackling fire once more. It was quiet heaven – or, perhaps, slightly noisy heaven, as the rain continued to lash down all around them, but without impinging on their happiness one jot . . .

'Anne was quite right, you know,' said George, once she had eaten most of her meal. There had been a rancorous

7

and ill-tempered mood all across Britain in the run-up to the EU referendum, and George felt appeased to be here, and to have all that behind her. Firelight flickered on her face. 'We can leave politics out of this. After all, if there's one thing that's stronger than politics, it's friendship. Right? We've never argued about it before, and we won't now.'

The others all nodded and smiled. And Timmy, who was fast asleep and chasing a fantastically delicious rabbit across a fabulous dreamscape, gave a soft, 'Woof!'

CHAPTER TWO

The First Debate

'That's just a load of calculating, self-serving horseshit!' shouted George.

'I say,' said Dick. 'Steady on!'

'I will *not* steady on,' George protested. 'This nonsense about not being able to get back to the mainland from here if we achieve independence, of emergency rescue services not visiting the island . . . And the implication that I am seeking to personally gain—'

'"Personally to gain",' said Julian, off to one side, studying his nails. 'Split infinitive.'

'You will personally gain my fist if you interrupt me one more time,' said George. Then she turned back to Anne and Dick. 'I'm appealing to your common sense. This is a measure which we all feel in our hearts – at least *I* do, and I think and hope you do too. And that means it's not just a step we should take, but one we *must* take. The campaigner on the other side is filling your heads with ridiculous threats

'Woof, woof!' said Timmy, a love of democracy running through him like an electric current. 'Woof!'

that will never come to pass. It's inconceivable that any of these things will happen. We need to make a stand about independence, because no one else will. And, therefore, I hope you join me when I say, "I'M OUT!"'

George sat back down, exhausted. She had never in her adult life spoken for so long and with such passion. And the result of her speech was clearly not unanimous – she could see uncertainty in Dick and Anne's faces. This referendum was certainly going to be a fight to the end . . .

Scarcely twenty-four hours had passed since their first meal on Kirrin Island, by the campfire.

Over the last few weeks, the lead-up to the British referendum on Europe had caused a spike in tension between George and Julian. Anne and Dick had been hoping this holiday would be the solution.

All the polls on television and in the newspapers had been saying all along that Britain was almost certainly going to vote to stay in the EU.

'Sticking with the status quo,' Julian had intoned miserably, every chance he got. 'Bunch of stupid sheep . . .'

Julian had a strong emotional response to the idea of Britain being in Europe: he hated it. And, perceiving that his side was going to lose, he had overlooked no opportunity to share his views with the group.

George fell naturally at the other end of the political spectrum and was sanguine at the prospect of Remaining. On being questioned about where she stood, Anne would politely point out it was a secret ballot, and she would like that to be respected. And Dick, never one to take sides, would point at Anne and say, 'Secret ballet . . . ballot . . . Whatever she said.'

(Timmy was considered to be neutral, although, if he had been capable of understanding the variety of sausages available on the European mainland, that could probably have been a deciding factor.)

The result of the referendum, when they woke up that morning in their rain-soaked camp in Kirrin Castle and discovered the news of it on their smartphones, had come as a shock to them all. Julian had made no attempt to hide his glee. He had spent the morning marching up and down the island (in so far as that was possible, considering the many puddles and marshy pockets) and declaring his bright hopes for the future.

George's temper had lasted until lunchtime, when Julian made one last smug peroration on freedom from the tyranny of Brussels, which proved the final straw. George went quiet as she typed something into her phone. Then she approached Julian and held the device up to him.

'Look,' she said. 'You want to know what my reaction is? Here.'

It was George's Twitter feed. Julian stared at it in puzzlement for a few moments before looking up.

'Your answer is a video of a baby panda playing a mouth organ?' he asked.

'Not that,' she said, pointing. '*That.*'

'Oh,' said Julian, reading. He looked up, squinted into the distance and thought about it for a moment. Then he said, 'Oh,' again, and sat down.

'What is it, Jules?' Anne asked.

'She's declared independence,' said Julian quietly.

'She's always been very independent,' said Dick, 'hasn't she? Why declare it now? Julian might as well declare on Twitter that he's—'

'*What*?' asked Julian.

'Nothing,' said Dick. 'Nothing at all. I wasn't going to say "obese". I was going to say "*not* obese". *Not* obese, Julian!' he repeated, as his older brother bore down upon him.

Meanwhile, Anne had taken the phone from Julian and looked at it herself.

'Oh dear,' she said. 'What Julian means is that George has declared independence for Kirrin Island. Because it is hers, so she can, I suppose . . .'

'From what?' asked Dick, distracted for a moment from fighting off Julian. 'From Europe? That doesn't make sens— *Ow*! Britain's already done that, hasn't it?'

'No,' said Anne. '*Stop that*, you two. She's declared independence from Britain!'

'I mean, she's only declared it to her 203 followers,' said Julian, letting go of Dick's throat. 'But still . . .'

'You mean . . . we're abroad?' Dick coughed. 'I haven't brought my passport!'

They looked around for George, but she was nowhere to be seen.

George had gone off in a huff.

This wasn't in itself anything new – her propensity for going off in huffs had been a major factor in her parents giving her the island in the first place. In her childhood, she had gone off in huffs so frequently that Aunt Fanny and Uncle Quentin had decided it would be helpful to give her a specific location with a natural boundary, so that, when in a huff, they most likely knew where George was.

This huff was, however, more potent than most. And, like many people in a sore temper, George had now said something that could not be taken back. But she meant it – by hell, she meant it. If Britain was to be so stupid and retrograde as to voluntarily leave such a broadly beneficial enterprise as the EU, then she wanted the country to know what she bloody well thought of it . . .

It was violent thoughts like these that accompanied her as she walked, eventually finding her way down to the beach that faced the mainland.

Then, looking out on the water, she spotted an object bobbing around a few hundred feet away: a small boat, with oars churning through the swell. She couldn't remember the last time the island had received visitors – that is, visitors in the daytime, who weren't coming here under the cover of darkness to hide some valuables, or engage in espionage or skulduggery.

She was not in the mood to be particularly welcoming, and, more for something to do than anything else, she sought along the beach until she found a satisfyingly large stick to wave.

'In case of bloody invaders,' she said to herself. 'I'm not going down in the *Guinness Book of Records* as having declared the briefest independence of all time . . .'

But by now the boat was near enough for George to recognize its crew. She climbed up on a rock to get a proper view, and so her voice would carry.

'Darling!' came her mother's voice. 'There you are!'

George suddenly experienced many feelings at once. She'd not seen her parents on this island since she was a child, and in the terrible mood she was in, she naturally felt grateful to set eyes on her mother. But in the same moment she had one of those flashes of cold, dreadful insight that only a person in a foul mood can access.

'WHICH WAY DID YOU VOTE?' she shouted.

Fanny and Quentin had clearly been expecting a more generous reception. There was the sound of muffled, puzzled conversation in the boat. The swell was not inconsiderable and, as the two occupants paused their rowing, the boat swung round.

'I'm sorry, darling, what?' called Aunt Fanny, putting a hand to her ear. Then she gasped and steadied herself against the boat's side.

'Don't try the helpless dodderer with me,' George

'Its so good to be out of London while all those disgusting toffs are deciding our future, and droning on about who's going to be in charge.'

muttered to herself. She knew full well that, having lived seven decades on the Dorset coast, her parents were extremely capable sailors. 'You heard me!' she shouted. 'Which way did you vote?'

'Is this really the time?'

Uncle Quentin, perceiving which way the conversation was going, began rowing again determinedly. Soon they were just a few yards away from the shore.

'Answer me!' yelled George.

'We aren't sure where Britain stands!' said Fanny.

'Answer in clear English, please,' said George. 'Which way?'

'We don't like having no control over our own laws!' Fanny went on. 'It's a matter of sovereignty! Please, darling; there was a power cut in the night, and the rain got in the back door – there's an inch of it all through downstairs. It's ghastly!'

'Go to town, then, and phone for someone.'

'We can't! Lightning struck a tree in the storm and it fell over the road, so we can't get to the mainland. Also, I'd made these delicious scones . . .'

'*You voted Brexit!*' George screamed.

The boat bobbed uncertainly on the waves. No answer came.

'Sorry – this island is full up!' said George, poking at the boat with her stick to try and turn it away. 'Go back where you came from!'

While this conversation had been going on, the others had come down from the castle to find George and talk to her. They were now wading into the water to help the boat ashore.

'Hey, Dick, Anne – I am your ruler and I *order* you not to help them.'

The others ignored her.

Throwing her stick into the swell, George jumped on to the sand and sped back up the beach towards the castle. If her parents wanted to drown themselves trying to enter the island illegally, they could jolly well go ahead.

My, she hadn't been in a temper like this for the longest time. Reaching the top of the beach, she stopped and stamped hard on the sand. George didn't remember the last time she'd stamped her feet in temper. But now she saw why people did it. It was mightily satisfying.

She marched at high speed back up to the castle ruins,

making some rapid decisions about the constitution of the new state of Kirrin Island. Capital punishment, she thought, was *definitely* not off the table . . .

Timmy, who had been following behind and wondering if he had done something wrong, abandoned her and ran back to the beach to dance around Aunt Fanny and Uncle Quentin, barking to his heart's delight.

CHAPTER THREE

Another Referendum

'*Another* referendum?' wailed Aunt Fanny.

'I'm afraid so, Mummy,' said George. 'I'm for leaving Britain, and Julian's for remaining in it. You see, once they caught wind that I'd declared independence, the other three all demanded citizenship – Dick, Anne and Julian – and I gave citizenship to Timmy, of course, without him asking. It seems only fair enough, because they were all residing on the island when I declared independence. And, of course, I can't imagine Kirrin Island without them.

'Then, when I'd admitted that, Julian said he didn't want the island to be independent, and that, because he made up twenty-five per cent of the human population, it was enough to trigger a referendum on the issue. I had to admit that was fair enough too.'

'But the first referendum upset people so!' said Aunt Fanny.

'Yet you voted the way you did,' said George.

'Just because I . . .' Aunt Fanny looked distraught. 'I didn't like people in Brussels deciding everything for us. I thought we should have power in Westminster. I didn't think it would actually happen . . .'

'Well, young lady,' said George firmly, 'you've got what you asked for. Some people are very upset. Don't come to me when you're unhappy with the outcome.'

The island was still considerably waterlogged, and unlikely to drain satisfactorily in the next few days, so the decision had been made to keep the camp where it was for the duration. Besides, Aunt Fanny commented, Anne had made it look so *nice*. Anne gave her a kiss.

The first debate had taken place shortly after lunch and, since it had broken down into squabbling, much of the rest of the afternoon was spent making up again afterwards, along with a failed search for dry camping ground. By the time room had been made in the camp for Aunt Fanny and Uncle Quentin, it was time for dinner.

Anne had asked politely if politics could once more be kept away from the dinner table, to which everyone agreed, a consensus made all the easier when Uncle Quentin revealed the hamper he had brought with him. It was an extremely lavish present from an old friend and colleague – a fellow scientist, who had moved to Europe and wished to show his appreciation for all Quentin had done for him. The scientist knew very well Uncle Quentin's adoration of cheese, and had sent a large selection of European varieties. Everyone oo-ed and aah-ed as each specimen was produced from the hamper and then spread or laid in slices upon biscuits. Gruyère from Switzerland, Cashel Blue from Ireland, Manchego from Spain, Italian Gorgonzola, Danish Blue, French Brillat-Savarin, Austrian Lüneberg and smoked Croatian Dimsi . . .

Now, soothed by the prospect of the treat in front of him, and replete in his smugness, Julian relaxed and made his fatal mistake. It was just after Dick was handed a cracker with a delicious slick of brie across it, to which Dick said, 'We must have made a rash decision, when the Europeans are capable of this . . .'

Julian replied, 'Oh, we can continue enjoying these delicacies, Dick – just, from afar. I, for one, am ecstatic to be free of the depredations of those unelected career bureaucra—'

'*That's it*,' said Anne. 'You have to go over there, Julian.

Timmy was neutral, although, if he had understood the variety of sausages available on the European mainland, that would have been a factor.

I'm sorry. Right over there, please. I asked nicely for zero politics, and you couldn't do it.'

Julian spluttered helplessly for a few moments, then saw in the eyes of everyone around the fire that he had overstepped the mark.

'You're not invited to be part of our party for the rest of the evening,' said Anne. 'If you enjoy these cheeses, it will have to be, as you put it, *from afar*. Perhaps you can think over your speech for the second debate tomorrow. This has got nothing to do with my politics, or anyone's, but you're deliberately disrupting the group. Do you agree, Dick?'

Dick nodded, avoiding Julian's gaze.

Losing her temper was an argumentative tactic Anne used only once in a blue moon, which was why it was so successful. Julian, too shocked to respond, quietly moved his sleeping bag to the far corner of the ruined castle chamber, where the floor was narrow and the drop-off steep, and where the reduced cover meant he was subject to occasional scatterings of rain.

Julian got in his sleeping bag and leant against the wall, looking for all the world like an oversized maggot who, unable to find work, had taken to begging. He felt that horrible mixture of emotion known to every punished schoolboy: one part indignation to three parts guilt. His self-recrimination was by no means mitigated by the fact he could hear everyone around the campfire speaking quietly to each other, their mood ruined almost as much as his.

He should have thought about his stump speech for the next day, but of course he couldn't take his mind away from the cheeses – which he loved so much more than Anne, Dick and George put together. He watched with a wrinkled nose as they guzzled them down without savouring their beautiful complexity, as he would have done.

And now he felt hungry. If he was to be denied food from mainland Europe, he'd jolly well eat something British. He rummaged in his bag and found a tin of beans. Well, I won't eat them cold, he thought. I haven't sunk that low. So, instead, he crawled to the edge of the fire (everyone pretending not to notice him) and placed the tin a few inches from a glowing log, where it would warm up nicely. He retreated to his spot of exile and thought about his speech for tomorrow.

Well, what could he say? What was there to argue about? This was just a heap of rock and Britain couldn't give two figs whether it stayed part of it or not – of that he was sure. He would debate on principles, he decided.

'Ah!' he said with considerable glee. The others looked over at him for a second, then turned back to their conversation. He had just remembered a treat he had packed to share with everyone. He rummaged in his rucksack and, retrieving it, sat back with it in his hands: a bottle of port. He tore the foil away with his teeth. Port and beans! He was sure many officers of the British navy had eaten far worse meals, on their long voyages. He felt bucked up.

Then there was a loud explosion, which made everyone jump and exclaim, including Timmy, who ran around the camp, woofing like his life depended on it. Dick soon discovered the culprit.

'Sorry, old chap,' he said to Julian, holding up the exploded Heinz can on a stick. 'You really should have opened it first.' It seemed the burning log had shifted closer and overheated the tin.

'No matter!' Julian called back to them, cheerfully. A dinner of a bottle of port, then, he thought, smothering his stomach's rumbling with a few glugs.

There was a steady drizzle, which did not seem to have

any intention of going away. Julian wriggled up and tried to go to sleep. And as he began to doze, he watched the others going to sleep, and kept one beady eye upon the unprotected Gorgonzola . . .

CHAPTER FOUR

Unexpected Turns of Events

'Anne?' said a gentle voice. 'Anne . . .'

She was aware of feeling cold, and having a painful bottom after rolling on to a pebble in her sleep, and of being unwilling to wake up. But this was a voice whose sound she adored so much that she opened her eyes at once.

Anne sat up, astounded. '*Dieter*,' she whispered, 'what are you *doing* here?'

Instead of responding, the German took her in his arms and kissed her. She gasped as he let go, and then glanced around nervously to see if the others were awakened. 'How did you find me?' she whispered, as quietly as she could. 'I . . . I say, it's jolly good to see you . . .'

They broke off their conversation to look into this kissing business with more energy and determination for a while, before pausing to speak once more.

'I have news for you, my dear one,' said Dieter. 'Such news! I am afraid to say it.'

'Oh, say it, Dieter! You can say anything to me,' she whispered. 'After all, we've been seeing each other for nearly a month now. We have no secrets!'

'I do not know how you voted, my dear Anne, and I shall not ask. But the worst has happened. Because Britain has voted for Brexit, I must leave. My company will no longer sponsor me staying in the country after this vote.'

'Are you sure?' Anne asked. 'Surely there is a chance you can appeal the decision!'

'I must leave you, my darling,' Dieter said, standing. 'I am sorry. I shall always miss you . . .'

'No, Dieter! Please! Don't go! Come back!'

But he had already disappeared into the shadows.

'Nooo!' yelled Anne, waking up with a start. Others stirred, but remained asleep. It was a very silly dream to have, she scolded herself. Like that of a teenage girl. She rubbed her stomach; she could feel the large amounts of undigested cheese there. Ah, that was it, she thought. She sat up and poked the glowing fire with a stick. Despite watching all the debates and assiduously reading the Sunday papers, Anne had been unsure, up to now, whether a Brexit vote would adversely affect her in any way. Gosh, how awful it had felt when he said it. She hugged her knees and looked

'Which way did you vote?' she shouted.

into the fire, thinking about serious Dieter, who had such lovely eyes.

She had not been sitting there long, when there was a loud grunt and George sat bolt upright, looking about crazily like a hunted animal. Then she seemed to understand where she was, and came to sit next to Anne, at the fire, while she got her breath back.

Not long afterwards, there was the sound of someone wriggling in their sleeping bag and Dick awoke with a yelp. Seeing the two girls nearby, he shuffled over to join them beside the fire.

'European-cheese dreams?' suggested Anne quietly, and the other two nodded.

They all watched the flames as the eastern sky started to lighten.

Eventually, Anne made coffee and they all sipped it. George thought about what she was going to say at the debate later. The other two thought about how much they were not looking forward to the debate later.

Suddenly, there came a '*Noooooo!*' from thirty feet away, at the other end of the stone floor.

The noise made Dick spit his coffee into the fire in

surprise, and turn to see his brother sitting up and panting, sweat standing out on his forehead. Dick saw the empty bottle of port next to Julian's sleeping bag. And he looked to where the cheeses had been put back and saw how depleted they were.

'Was that you, Timmy?' Dick asked. 'Attacking the cheeses while we were asleep? Naughty Timmy!'

'Woof!' Timmy said, indignantly.

CHAPTER FIVE

The Second Debate

The debate was set for midday, and carried with it such a sense of occasion that Uncle Quentin and Aunt Fanny felt they had to stay and watch. Julian had brought a Union Jack flag with him that he had intended to hang from the battlements in angry defiance when the UK decided to remain in the EU. Now, however, he would be waving it in the spirit of joyful patriotism, to try and persuade Kirrin Island to remain part of the UK. He was bustling about, muttering under his breath and preparing his speech. Suddenly, he turned to George.

'The country will be called Kirrin Island, George, will it?' he asked.

'I suppose so. The island is barely larger than the average supermarket car park, so we can hardly call it Great Kirrin.'

'Small Kirrin, then,' said Dick.

'Pocket Kirrin?' asked Anne.

'Kirrin Island,' said George firmly. 'And there are various other decisions I've made about it too, but I'll come to them later. First, it's time for this beastly debate.'

'I'm ready!' said Julian.

Everyone sat on blankets on the grass in front of a stretch of stone battlements that would serve as a podium. George and Julian stood on this, about five feet away from each other, and faced the electorate.

'Now,' George said, 'Julian and I will each give a brief speech, and then we will throw the debate open for questions. Julian, over to you.'

Julian was in his element. It's not entirely in the interests of the reader to repeat his whole speech here, only to say that, to his own ears, it was soaring, emotional, and contained something of the majesty and bombast of Churchill at his best. To the others, however, it was silly, over the top, pompous and repetitive. His main point was about the greatness of Britain, and how – now it was free from the shackles of Europe and able to follow its own destiny – Kirrin would be mad to detach itself from the mother country and make itself a small, cold, pointless outpost. In the tradition of public speakers everywhere, he said what he was going to say, then he said it, and he was in the middle

She couldn't remember the last time the island
had received visitors.

of saying it again when everyone yelled at him to shut up, and Uncle Quentin threw a cupcake at his head.

He stepped down to a smattering of polite applause from Aunt Fanny and Anne, and George took over.

'As you know, I want Kirrin Island to become independent from the UK,' she started. 'Kirrin Island belongs to me, so you should bloody well go along with what I say, and that's that. Questions?'

Anne put her hand up at once. 'I understand how you both feel about it – that's clear. But what will actually happen to Kirrin Island if it *does* become independent?'

'A very good question, Anne,' said Julian sorrowfully. 'I fear the consequences could be quite dreadful. Imagine this beautiful place being cut off completely from the mainland . . .'

'It *is* cut off, you berk,' sighed George. 'It's an island. That's why we like it.'

'The fishing rights that would be lost,' said Julian. 'The administrative nightmare of crossing from one country to another every time we want to go to the shops, or for a bike ride? I fear the red tape needed even to grant ourselves legal passports could bankrupt the economy and render the island inaccessible, even to us!'

Anne and Dick nodded, taking this in. It did seem plausible.

'After all, we should be grateful to be free of the bureaucracy of the European Union! A barmy place. Just listen to some of these perfectly crazy EU bans: references to non-Halal meats in Christmas-cracker jokes; sun cream for the epileptic; reheating quiche; exchanging gifts in a hot-air balloon; alcoholic picnics on chalky soil; freewheeling on a tandem; storing nutmeg in a confined space; storing nutmeg in the open air; operating a funeral parlour while colour blind; the use of bald ornamental dice; sarcastic apologies.'

'Those things aren't true!' protested George. 'He's making it all up!'

'And I'm sorry to say this,' Julian went on, 'but I fear there could be a profit motive in this so-called "principled" independence bid. After all, how many times have we discovered hidden maps, smuggled goods or crucial military intelligence on this island – each of them with enormous potential worth on the open market? After independence, these items would no longer belong to the crown, but to a certain Ms Kirrin, who would stand to make an incalculable fortune from them!'

George could see the crowd turning against her. She normally liked people turning against her, as it gave her something to fight against. But this game of stealth and politics, this war of hearts and minds, was completely alien to her. She felt as helpless as a seal trying to play table tennis – or 'pash-pish'. She flailed for a response while the electorate stared upon her with chilly suspicion.

'Look,' George said, 'no one cares about this island except us. There's no risk to fishing quotas, because there are no fishing quotas. There will be no loss of revenue because there is no revenue. The flowers will bloom and the rabbits – yes, Timmy, "woof!" indeed – will run about, and all will carry on as before. But it will be independent. I really believe in this, and I hope you do too.'

Anne and Dick and Aunt Fanny all clapped half-heartedly.

'Hear, hear!' said a loud voice behind them.

They turned to see a slick-looking man in a pinstripe suit (and wellingtons, owing to the mud) applauding. If there was anything that could have robbed George of her decorum after delivering her little speech, it was his arrival. Even Aunt Fanny, catching sight of him, let out a dismayed gasp.

'Oh, good gracious, Rupert!' Fanny said. 'How you crept up on us! How did you get here? And what the devil are *you* doing on Kirrin?'

CHAPTER SIX

Kirrin Gets a PR Man

While Julian, George, Dick and Anne had their differences, they had always fought for what they collectively knew to be right. And whatever that cause was, their older cousin, Rupert, who they had only really come to know in adulthood, always seemed to fall on the opposite side of it. Wherever they encountered dishonesty, corruption, profiteering or mendacity, they soon afterwards discovered that he was somehow involved. And no matter how hard they tried to put him behind bars once and for all, sooner or later he slithered out of their grip.

Here and now, however, there were various things to be said for not immediately trussing him up like a turkey and flinging him into the castle dungeon.

The first was the fact that Kirrin had only been proposed as an independent country for about twenty-four hours, and nobody wanted the first executive action in the country's history to be locking someone up without evidence or due

41

Dick was handed a cracker with a delicious slick of brie across it. 'We must have made a rash decision, when the Europeans are capable of this . . .' he observed.

process – whatever the temptation. Besides, he was broad and tall, and would take some imprisoning.

The second was the speech he made to the group (after first explaining he had reached the island by a new water-taxi service, called Uboat).

Standing there, looking like several thousand pounds' worth of London tailoring, he removed his sunglasses and said, 'Guys. I know we've had our differences in the past. I won't deny it. But I've observed that this situation is blowing up in a way you don't yet understand. Kirrin Island and its independence is about to become a big story. You are going to need someone who knows how to talk to the press. Not to mention some serious lawyers. And I know some *serious* lawyers. You're looking at me like I'm mad. Have you not looked at the TV in the last few hours?'

'Of course,' said Julian. 'We've had our sixty-four-inch flat-screen tuned to News 24 from the moment we arrived on this remote island without electricity.'

'Well, check Twitter, then.'

They all (except for Quentin and Fanny) looked at their phones. After a moment, George swore violently – and immediately apologized to her parents.

'What is it, darling?' asked Fanny.

43

'When George made the announcement on Twitter yesterday, she had 203 followers,' said Dick.

'That's an awful lot,' said Aunt Fanny. 'You must be very proud, darling!'

'She now has 425,000 followers,' said Anne.

Aunt Fanny opened and closed her mouth several times, accompanying each opening and closing with a different thoughtful expression. 'What does it mean?' she finally asked.

'It means Kirrin Island is news,' said Rupert. 'And we should all get ready . . .'

Once Cousin Rupert had finished briefing her, George nodded.

'Okay,' she said, turning to the others. 'Now, this is what you should all know: despite wanting to stay here on our own and have a nice quiet time, lots of people are going to come. That's right, isn't it, Rupert?'

Rupert nodded.

'Camera crews and journalists, quite possibly,' George went on, 'and if they manage to get close enough, they'll ask you all questions. I'm sorry about that. Please, just refer them to me. Or play stupid. Can you manage that, Dick?'

'Oh, yes.'

'Good. And I'll do my best to field the questions. By the way,' George said, 'I have been neglecting my duties as head of state, allowing hours to pass without announcing my Cabinet. So, if you are ready and willing to serve, Dick, I would like to make you Minister of the Interior.'

'Oh, that's nice, Dick,' said Aunt Fanny. 'Well done!'

'What is that, exactly?' Dick asked. 'I mean, I'm terribly grateful, of course.'

'It is an utterly vital position,' said George, 'and I will brief you on your specific tasks later.'

Dick nodded.

'Julian,' George went on, 'I would like to appoint you Minister in charge of Island Security – if you'll accept the post.'

Julian was appalled that George was engaging in open bribery – or flattery, at least – to win over the electorate. But he couldn't deny his pride at the appointment. 'I shall serve with all my strength,' he said, saluting.

'Anne,' George said, 'I'd like you to be Home Secretary.'

'Lovely,' said Anne. 'I fully intend to be the best Home Secretary Kirrin Island has ever had.'

'I'm sure you will be, darling,' said Aunt Fanny.

'How about the military, or the air force?' asked Julian. At that moment, a butterfly alighted for a second on his nose.

'There's your air force,' said George, as Julian twitched his nose and the butterfly floated above their heads. 'I appoint her. Now, Timmy!'

'Woof!' said Timmy, bounding over.

'I want you to be Attorney General,' said George.

'Woof!' said Timmy.

'With special responsibility for sausages.'

'Woof! Woof!'

'Now, give me a kiss; I'm depressed.'

'Woof!' said Timmy, slathering her with affection.

CHAPTER SEVEN

Population Explosion

Although they had been warned to expect an influx of journalists, evening came with no sign of them, and everyone
went to bed quietly around the fire, albeit with a sense of
foreboding. The ground on the island was still not yet dry
enough to pitch camp on, and Fanny and Quentin had gone
home and brought back some items for Julian and enough
spare blankets to make everyone comfortable.

Early next morning, George was woken by Anne, next to
her, writhing in her sleep. She made an indistinct exclama-
tion of wrenching emotion. 'No,' she said. 'No, Fernando,
don't go! We can sort something out with the Spanish
embassy ... Please ...' Then she rolled over and went
back to sleep, leaving George awake with nothing to do
but worry about the situation and what would become of
all this. She had declared independence in order to get shot
of everyone, yet that very act had got her enmeshed with
all sorts of people she would dearly love to avoid.

When a vague smell of salty meat drifted over the camp, George dismissed it at first as an olfactory hallucination. But, a few minutes later, she caught the unmistakeable smell of fried onions coming from somewhere. Still groggy, she pulled on her jeans and her boots, and went off to investigate.

Half awake, George stumbled down through the rocks, on to the beach, where she found herself standing in front of an unaccountable apparition.

'Wanna hotdog, love?' said a man, standing next to a hotdog stall.

'For breakfast?' she asked.

'Why not?' he said. He was about fifty, tall and bald, plump around the middle, and he introduced himself as Bernie.

'What are you doing here?' George asked.

'I'll be honest with ya.' He shrugged. 'I normally work on the seafront at Weymouth in the summer. But the weather's been so rotten, when I saw on the news about this place, I rowed out here to set up.'

'You know what? Yes, please, I will have one,' said George. She fished in her pocket for coins.

'Onions?' said the man.

48

'The island is barely larger than the average supermarket car park, so we can hardly call it Great Kirrin.'

'Go on, then,' said George. 'But surely the seven of us won't keep you busy?'

'Oh, I didn't come for you, darling,' he said cheerfully, and pointed over her shoulder at the beach. 'I came for them.'

George turned and, looking again at the beach, was staggered to find that what she'd thought, when she'd seen it out of the corner of her eye, to be an enormous bank of seaweed was in fact several dozen inhabited sleeping bags, as well as countless further packs of equipment. There were also a few dinghies scattered about here and there.

'Who are they?' George asked.

'Journalists,' said Bernie. 'They arrived in the night.'

'Bloody hell,' said George, and, thanking the man for his hotdog, she ran back to the castle ruins. By the time she got there, the others were all roused and making themselves breakfast. George told them what she'd seen, and they sipped their morning tea in forced quiet, trying to relish their final moment of peace.

Rather than get hijacked by the journalists when it pleased them, George decided to hold a press conference, nice and early, to make her feelings clear. She made sure everyone had been given a breakfast hotdog and cup of tea or coffee beforehand (by sunup, Bernie's cousin, Terence, had arrived with a coffee stall). Then she took a deep breath and invited the first question.

'First, may I ask what the name of the new country is?' asked a journalist.

'Kirrin Island.'

'A touch vainglorious, perhaps? Naming it after yourself?'

'Of course not,' she snapped. 'It's always been called Kirrin Island, going back hundreds of years. I couldn't tell you what was named first, my family or it. But we share the name, yes.'

'What is the minimum voter turnout for the result to be binding?' asked a different reporter.

'Four voters,' said George.

'Uh-huh. And what is the maximum turnout you are expecting?' asked another.

'Four voters,' said George. 'And a dog.'

There was murmuring in the crowd, and other reporters raised their hands. 'Georgina Kirrin,' one began.

'It's *George*,' said George. Standing behind her, Rupert winced.

'George, sorry. I understand you don't actually live on the island?'

'No,' George admitted. 'No one does, except some rabbits – shush, Timmy! You don't have to bark each time I say "rabbits", for heaven's— *Shush!*'

'Some people might say this is a ruse to avoid tax, that you are just declaring independence to give yourself and your friends "non-dom" status. What do you say to that?'

'I say why don't you wait for those people to say that, then introduce me to them and see whether they still think it at the end of the conversation?' said George aggressively.

'Calm . . . Calm . . .' urged Rupert over her shoulder.

'Well, another charge being levelled at you is that you have no plan. Post . . . well, perhaps I should say "Post-Krexit"?'

George shuddered at this extraordinarily ugly neologism.

'No plan?' she asked. 'I mean . . . look at it. It's a tiny island with no roads, running water or electricity. What do you want me to do? Build a leisure centre for shrews and voles? Do *shush*, Timmy.'

'So you're admitting you have no clear plan for the island's future?'

'Pardon me,' George said, her voice becoming danger-ously quiet. 'I do indeed have a clear plan. I plan for plants to grow, and the tides to wash on the beaches, and for time to go about its business, until we've all died of old age and there's no one to bother about on the island except the rabbits. *Shut up*, Timmy!'

George was starting to get a sharp headache behind her eyes and, as her press agent, Rupert perceived that her already short temper was really beginning to fray. So he stepped in, thanked everyone for their questions, and said that was all for now.

As Rupert continued to wrap things up with the press, George turned and began to walk away, towards the castle, glummer than ever. Timmy caught up with her and she ruffled his head, all instantly forgiven on both sides. But as he scampered off ahead, her bad temper returned and she trudged up the hill, making faces about the word 'Krexit'.

Rupert caught up with her a minute later.

'I'm sorry to say that we're already on the defensive,' he said. 'While you were doing that, Julian's been making strides to get his opinion in the press. He's already been on BBC Radio Solent, Wessex FM and Broadchurch Digital.'

*'It **is** cut off, you berk,' sighed George. 'It's an island. That's why we like it!'*

'But really, Rupert, who cares about this tiny island?' George said. 'Or, at least, *why* do they care?'

'Oh, they won't in a week's time; I guarantee you that,' said Rupert. 'But, for now, you're the story of the moment. And you must try to put across the right message, while you've got everyone's attention.'

'What's in this for you, Rupert?' George asked. 'Why have you come to help me?'

Rupert appeared shocked.

'Don't forget I grew up not far from here, myself,' he said. 'My name's Kirrin too, remember. When I saw what was happening, I knew that I had expertise that you didn't, in these matters, and I could see how things might easily go wrong. I wanted to come down and help you to avoid making a mess of the situation. Not to mention the family name.'

'Okay,' George said. 'I'm sorry, Rupert. It's very kind of you; I do appreciate it . . .'

But even before he could accept her apology, Rupert had turned away to answer a call.

CHAPTER EIGHT

A Kind Word

'Stupid Julian and his stupid politics,' George muttered, kicking a stone ahead of her as she walked along the beach on the other side of the island, as far away from the crowd as she could be. Kicking the stone again with all her might, she jumped as she watched it skitter across the pebbles and thump into the leg of her father, as he was bent over a small rowing boat.

'What's going on?' he asked as he span round, rubbing his calf.

'Sorry, Daddy!' she said. 'I didn't expect anyone to be here, so I wasn't looking. I was rather caught up in my own thoughts.'

'Don't worry,' he said, letting go his calf and looking her up and down. She certainly seemed quite miserable. 'Get in,' he said. 'We're going fishing. I think you and I should talk.'

'There *must* be something wrong with the world,' George

replied, climbing aboard, 'when my dad volunteers to speak to me. Are horses riding humans, and fish swimming in the sky?'

Quentin clambered in after her and set the oars. 'Shut up for a minute,' he said, 'and take one of these oars.'

Peace descended on the boat as they rowed, side by side, until they were clear of the beach. The physical exercise soothed George's bad temper, as did the rhythmic slapping of the waves, and the squeak and knock of the oars. Quentin said they were to row round to the other side of the island, where the fishing was better.

'Well . . . So, it was your mother's idea that we speak,' Quentin admitted at last. He bid her give the second oar to him and sit up front, so they could look at each other while they spoke. 'I know this is all awful at the moment,' he said, when she was sitting down again, 'but, whatever the outcome, it won't be the end of the world. After all, you don't mean to live on Kirrin forever, do you?'

'Of course not,' George said. 'But someone has to make a statement. Don't they? Because I feel this issue *very* strongly, Daddy. Really, I do.'

'I certainly admire you for making a stand,' said Quentin, 'having never been very politically minded myself. And, as a parent, I know I've never been very . . . very communicative. Do you know why that is?'

George shook her head.

'Because I love you and approve of you – in everything you do. I think you're a good person. If you displeased me, then you'd better believe you'd know about it.' He flashed a smile – not at her, exactly, but at a seagull cawing overhead. 'But you don't. I honestly feel you're the best daughter a father could have. Just promise me,' Quentin went on, regaining his customary sternness, 'you won't let all this political nonsense ruin things – ruin this island, but, more importantly, ruin the special bond between you and the others.'

George was profoundly moved by this little speech, and didn't feel able to respond with any more than a nod.

'Wait a minute,' Quentin said, letting go of the oars with a gasp. 'I haven't rowed this boat for forty years. I wonder if . . .' He reached under his seat, and then hammered at a supporting plank. When it came loose, he laughed with glee. 'Ha ha!' he said. 'Would you know it? It's still here!'

George looked at him as though he had lost his mind. Then she too gasped, as he withdrew his hand, because in it was a bottle of whiskey.

'What the hell?' asked George.

'Ah, you see,' said Quentin, pulling out the cork with his teeth. 'When I was courting your mother, her father was rather a solemn, distant man. Hated young people and didn't trust them.'

'I can only imagine what that was like,' said George.

'And the only times I ever had a chance to really . . . you know, *get to know* your mother . . .'

'Oh, *please*, Daddy, spare me the—'

'. . . was when I rowed her out here. So we used to sit on the beach and watch the sunset, and have a little tipple, and a bit of a cuddle . . .'

'Let me try some,' said George, and, taking the half-empty bottle, she took a sip from it. 'Wow,' she said, looking at the label and coughing. 'What an unexpected way for you to reveal your human side . . .' She held it up and took another sip.

'Give it back!' said Quentin, making to grab the end of the bottle, but she swung it free of his hand, without taking it away from her mouth. 'Damn it, you're my daughter, aren't you?' he said. 'All right, that's enough! Don't drink it all!'

At that moment, Julian was on the other side of the castle, looking out to sea. He had just rung off from yet another interview in which he believed he had comported himself really rather well. From this spot, he had a wonderful view out into the channel, which was choppy and grey-green beneath a vast cloudy sky. He had long secretly desired to become a Conservative MP one day, and this referendum was turning out to be a highly stimulating first political challenge, he thought. He looked out on the view with satisfaction.

'Dear nephew,' said a voice, disturbing Julian's reverie. He turned to find Aunt Fanny standing a few feet behind.

'Dearest aunt!' he said.

'Will you walk with me?' she asked, to which he, of course, assented.

'I'm worried about this referendum of yours,' Aunt Fanny said, before they'd gone half a dozen paces.

'Why so, dear F.?' asked Julian.

'You see, I know it matters to you so – the idea of it. But if you both follow your principles and fight to the death . . . Why, you see there's bound to be a winner and a loser.'

'Yes,' said Julian.

'And . . .' Fanny sighed and looked up at the sky. 'The

*'So you're admitting you have no clear plan
for the island's future?'*

reason this has come about is because the referendum – the one in *Britain*, I mean – divided people so terribly. I've been listening to stories on the radio of families torn apart, friends – even married couples – not speaking.'

'Yes, I see,' said Julian, not seeing.

'This Kirrin independence business has come about because of all that division. And yet it threatens to do the same thing all over again – to you young people.'

'Do you think we should not stand up for what we believe in?' asked Julian.

'Naturally, you should,' said Aunt Fanny unhappily. 'I would never ask you to do otherwise. And when you're young, you feel these idealistic things so much harder in your heart. But when you become a parent, things change. I wish I could make you understand.'

'I'm trying to understand,' said Julian.

'When you've reached my elevated age, you will see, Julian, that there is nothing more important than family, or the ties of friendship. There are millions of people who would *kill* to have experienced the close friendship you four have shared – *five*, I mean, including dear Timmy. Just think about that, I beg you, before you do something that harms your friendship irreparably.'

'I will,' said Julian, his jauntiness vanishing by the second.

'She is my daughter, yet it's you I am asking,' said Aunt Fanny. 'I've not admitted this to anyone, Julian, but I have always wondered if I was quite the right mother for George. She was such a *specific* child. I always wanted everyone just to be happy, and yet everything I said seemed to infuriate her. But when she met you and Anne and Dick, she was transformed. She loved you so much. And from an angry, insular child, she became this confident, happy, fearless person. And I think she changed all of you, too. *That* is why I'm asking, dear Julian.'

'I promise,' said Julian, his voice feathered with emotion.

They walked on a few more paces in silence. Then Fanny gasped.

'Oh, my!' she said. They had wandered into a corner of the castle ruins, where the walls were largely covered with moss. 'Let's see if it's still here . . .' Aunt Fanny muttered to herself as she stooped down and waggled a piece of loose rock.

Julian watched her distractedly as he thought about what she'd said, not even taking notice when she gave a little yelp as the rock came free in her hand, revealing a gap.

'What on earth are you doing?' Julian asked.

'You see,' Fanny said, as she rooted around in the hole with her arm, 'forty years ago, when we were courting, Uncle Quentin was terrified of my father. So he used to row me out here, ply me with whiskey and try to have his wicked way, the filthy beast. That's why I hid this!'

To Julian's astonishment, in her hand was a cricket bat.

'If he went too far, I was going to hit him with this!' she said. She swished it through the air and Julian retreated, ducking, and marvelling at how someone can reveal so many new sides of themselves, in just a few minutes.

'I've got to go – it's time for my press conference,' Julian said. 'I've got preparation to do.'

'First, I'd give him a whack on the ribs,' said Aunt Fanny, dancing ahead of him, wielding the cricket bat like a samurai sword. 'Then a strong bash over the head . . .'

CHAPTER NINE

The World According to Julian

Although overcast and somewhat dull by Dorset standards, when the journalists gathered on the shore just before lunch-time, there was something of a party atmosphere. As a rule, they were used to working in offices, or – more likely, these days – from home, and finding themselves corralled together at the edge of a beach on the south coast, ready to hear the political address of a crackpot West Country separatist, they were somewhat giddy and high-spirited.

After keeping them waiting for just a few minutes while he pinned the Union Jack around his neck to wear as a cape, Julian rose to stand on the top of a tall, jagged rock face that blocked off one end of the beach, and addressed the crowd.

'Good morning, ladies and gentlemen,' he said. 'I would like to tell you all about my vision for Kirrin Island. Then I will throw it open for questions.

'My campaign is based on hope. Hope for the future.

Hope for the possibilities of this beautiful island. The eyes of the world are focused on Kirrin, and with that there are manifold opportunities, which could bring investment of tens of millions of pounds. These include tourism, fishing rights and naming rights, to mention just a few. After all, we have a magnificent castle and a picturesque shipwreck. Why not rename them the Hunger-Buster Burger™ Castle Experience – a house of horrors combined with a rock-climbing centre? And perhaps the Clent's Original Dorset Ginger Beer™ Interactive Pirate Adventure – involving snorkelling tours and treasure-hunting trips? There is paper-work to be done, of course, but, at a conservative estimate, there are three hundred and fifty million pounds' worth of opportunities to be exploited here – money which could trickle down into the pockets of the ordinary residents of Dorset!'

The assembled journalists took this in for a moment.

'My opponent wants this independence to be a gesture,' said Julian. 'And I'll show you what sort. You see this rock I am standing on? You know what we Kirrinites call this?'

Naturally, the journalists didn't, and in a collective murmur said so.

'Because we have no lavatories, this is called the *toilet*

rock. And it's this rock that George Kirrin wants to throw us all off. She thinks Britain has already gone down the toilet, so she feels this small but beautiful island should too!'

With that forcefully expressed finale, Julian refused to answer any questions (despite his earlier promise) and said he would speak to the journalists again later today. Then took two steps left, and launched himself down a zip wire he had erected an hour earlier (from a length of rope he'd found in the castle) in order to make a dashing exit. For a few seconds, he did indeed swoop impressively over the heads of the crowd, with the flag flying behind him, but he had not fixed the further end of the zip line quite low enough and so, as the rope sagged under his weight, he slowed to an embarrassing halt, hanging above the journalists.

'Bally nuisance, what?' he said, dangling just over their heads, the wind blowing his hair back and forth. Beneath him, professional photographers snapped and snapped away. 'I don't suppose anyone would give me a push?' he asked.

The only response he got was hundreds of click-click-clicking noises.

'I guess I'm hanging here for a bit,' Julian admitted, reaching into his shirt. 'Lucky I brought a tin of good old British corned beef to keep me companeeeAAARGH—'

As the rope sagged under his weight,
Julian slowed to an embarrassing halt.

George, who had been watching with a dispassionate eye, had severed the line.

In the middle of the day, one or two journalists came up to the camp, where the family were going about their business. One of them approached Dick and asked if he would answer some questions.

'I'd much rather you spoke to George,' he said.

'You're not George?' the reporter asked. 'I only just got here . . .'

'No!' said Dick. 'George is a girl.'

'Ah. Then, if you don't mind, Miss Kirrin,' said the reporter, turning to Anne.

'For heaven's sake – that's George, over there,' said Anne, pointing at George, on the other side of the camp, who had found the whole exchange highly amusing. The reporters came directly over to her.

'Do you have any answer to your cousin's arguments?' one of them asked, after relaying some of Julian's points.

'Not really,' said George. 'He's talking such rubbish, it's not worth dignifying with an answer. Why do you ask?'

'He's been talking about not triggering Article 92 for two years, even if the vote goes against him,' said the reporter.

'Whoop-de-whiddle-de-doo,' George said. 'What does that mean?'

'Article 92 regulates the length and plumpness of broccoli florets in salads served to guests of the Polish State Carnival.'

'Huh.' George smiled. 'Well, why don't you ask him about that?'

'I will,' promised the reporter.

Julian's next speech to the assembled press was at 2 p.m. This time, he took a leaf out of George's book. Where she had given the press corps teas and coffees, Julian had smuggled ashore several multi-litre plastic jugs of home-made Dorset cider, purchased from a farmhouse, and distributed it among the journalists in paper cups. He wanted to encourage the jolly atmosphere he'd noticed among them and, of course, he was keen to enamour himself to them, after the morning's calamitous mishap.

When he was sure most of them had received a drink, Julian quickly climbed into his boat and checked that the slogans hanging off the side were well presented. Parading his slogans in front of them while giving his speech was, he thought, taking Kirrin politics to the next level – and a bit of good old fashioned showmanship. He had made two banners saying *TAKE BACK CONTROL* and *Independence Day!* before remembering those were his Brexit slogans, and that, in this battle, he was on the other side. In the end, he had settled for a sign that read *Kirr*IN, which he thought was rather snappy.

After checking in a pocket mirror that his suit and tie looked presentable, he rowed out into the swell. The tide was not strong and he soon turned the boat around to face the shore, taking care that everyone on the beach could see him. Standing, he lifted his megaphone and thanked them all for being there, and began his speech.

He spoke at length about his passion and commitment to the cause, while making, of course, the exact same arguments he had been making all along, in slightly different words. He could not resist, either, getting in another dig at the EU.

'Let's not forget the bureaucratic nightmare of the EU – an organization that has no fewer than 214 laws covering the production of raspberry jam! And the ridiculous fruits they foisted upon us – Frankenfruits, I call them. Straight bananas. Saggy plums. Round melons, firm cherries, hard cucumbers . . . Sorry, I lost my train of thought. Any questions?'

It seemed the liquor he had distributed had, for the moment, sharpened rather than dimmed the press's inquisitiveness. And the twenty yards' distance between them didn't matter, as it was such a calm day he could clearly hear their questions, without shouting. The £350 million stipend was called into question, which line of enquiry Julian hotly rebuked, while refusing to reveal how he had reached the figure. He assured the journalists it was based on sound economic projections.

Then the journalist who had spoken to George politely made his comment about the nature of Article 92. Julian handled it superbly.

'I apologize,' Julian said, chuckling into his megaphone. 'I'm only human. I can't boast the entirety of European law at my fingertips, and I'm sure there are few who can.' He beamed, an expression so uncharacteristic that it made Aunt Fanny and Anne, who were watching from the beach, look away. 'I think I meant Article 114,' he said.

'Really,' he went on, 'all this reliance on facts and experts is, I think, deeply patronizing to the average Kirrin voter. They've had enough of *experts*.' He spat the word as though it nearly made him vomit. 'They know the *real* facts, deep down. They know how they *feel*, and I think, when voting day comes round, they will vote with their feet!'

'Or paws,' called out one reporter.

'Or, indeed, paws,' conceded Julian. 'Listen,' he went on in a tone of disbelief, 'my opponent doesn't even think that Kirrin Island should be on email. You simply *have* to be on email these days! Does anyone here disagree? I thank you!'

And, so saying, he was about to sit down and row victoriously to the shore, when a fish hit him over the head. He staggered on his feet – the boat wobbled – and, as he regained his composure, he heard a few journalists calling out claims of sabotage. Julian turned to see George and Uncle Quentin in a boat not far behind him. George held a fish in her arms, and they both wore expressions of startled guilt.

It was at this point Julian remembered the props he had packed and forgotten to use. This was a bag of British foods with protected status that he had been hoping to make a point with – perhaps by eating them in front of the crowd of journalists. Reaching into the bag, he pulled out a Melton Mowbray pork pie and lobbed it with satisfying precision at his uncle's head, against which it broke into two halves.

On the other boat, George and Quentin were completely

bewildered by this turn of events. Quentin had already landed a good number of juicy fish, enough to feed them on the island for the next few days, but had just decided one of them was not large enough to keep, so had flung it back into the water as far as he could throw. It was only when he caught sight of Julian, and immediately afterwards copped a pie to the head, that he realized there was a problem.

'Pathetic attempt to undermine my campaign!' Julian yelled through his megaphone. 'Have this!' He flung a Cumberland sausage at them, which George, picking up an oar, thumped far into the sea, baseball style. This raised a cheer from Aunt Fanny and Anne.

This sight of sausages being used as missiles, combined with the alcohol finally seeping into their veins, stirred the collected journalists to action. Dick had been passing among them and handing out free hotdogs for the last half hour, intended to soak up the booze. Instead, these were suddenly launched into the air. They were not launched with universally brilliant aiming, however, so, as occupants of both boats looked up, they saw a sky made grey with incoming frankfurters, as though they were on the losing side at a watery Agincourt.

All members of the flotilla shielded themselves as the

'He's been talking about not triggering Article 92,'
said the reporter.
'Whoop-de-whiddle-de-doo,' George said.

fusillade rained in and the boats filled thumpingly with sausages. Then it was open season. Although Julian took to his megaphone to decry the people in the other boat, he also turned to shout at those on the shore. He was equally indiscriminate when it came to throwing the precious British products he had brought – his wedge of Dorset Blue Vinny, his Cornish pasty, his tin of Gloucester rice pudding, his Rutland toffee apple – but he kept his bottle of Plymouth gin, telling himself he might have to sterilize a wound with it. George stuck her head over the rim to holler insults, and to throw frankfurters and fish back at Julian and the shore.

'Retreat!' called Quentin, taking oars. Ignoring the non-vegetarian missiles flying at the boat, with a few dozen heaves he managed to get them out of danger, and then off, around the edge of the island.

When Julian finally made it ashore, looking rather haggard, he tried to make it an heroic entrance. He loosened his collar and tie, and accepted a can of beer from Dick, who was under strict instructions to be on hand to give it to him. Then he passed dozens of beers out to the assembled journalists and circulated with them, making sure he was photographed as often and from as many angles as possible, drinking beer and smiling. He lit a cigarette and held it in his fingers while he smiled broadly for the cameras, even though he detested smoking, or even having one of these beastly things near him. But it had to be done for politics.

After the battle of the flotilla, a holiday mood prevailed among the group on the beach. Julian was growing dizzy with success, when he was approached by the same troublesome reporter as before, who explained to him that Article 114, which he had quoted, in fact regulated the viscosity of lubricant used in the steel chains on cattle-bearing funiculars in the north and north-easterly states of Austria. Julian could not afford to lose face in front of the cameras.

'Let's be completely honest about this,' he said, smiling. '*Krexit means Krexit*.' And, with a pint of beer in one hand, he punched the air with the other. Alcohol was now holding sway, and his announcement garnered a small cheer. 'Krexit means Krexit!' he said again. 'It does! It means it! Yes!'

CHAPTER TEN

The Ballot Box

When George got back to the main camp in the castle ruins, she climbed up to the top and looked down at the beach, trying to see how many journalists there were. To her surprise, she saw it wasn't only journalists who were gathering; there were little boats coming across from the mainland all the time, disgorging tourists, day trippers – or temporary immigrants – whatever you wanted to call them. Looking through Quentin's binoculars, she saw there were now people on the beach selling ice cream and offering face painting. Someone had even set up a phone-recharging stall. George decided this was definitely getting out of hand. (But she also made a mental note to remind everyone to visit that stall in case their batteries ran out.)

When she had a chance to catch up with Julian, George did her best to ignore how much he was glowing with success, and begged for the vote to be as soon as possible, so all this could be over and done with. Julian agreed without hesitation. It was practically tea time now, so they fixed to have the vote the following morning.

Then, as George peeled away from the main group, Rupert approached her.

'There's someone very special I want you to meet,' he said.

'Fine,' George said automatically. 'Do I need to be nice to them?'

'Don't worry about that,' said Rupert, guiding her to the door in the castle wall that led down to the dungeons. 'I've found a space for you to talk in private.' Rupert walked George down the lengthy stone spiral staircase and, at the bottom, took her to the nearest dungeon cell.

Inside, she found lit candles spaced around the chamber and, in the centre, a table boasting cups and a cafetière. Behind it, a man: a slim, almost cadaverous man of late middle age. She first caught sight of him sipping coffee with his pinky extended – a gesture which made him look both delicate and diabolical. After introducing them to each other (the man's name was Princewell), Rupert vanished into the darkness.

'No doubt Rupert has explained what my visit is about,' said Mr Princewell.

'Quite the opposite,' said George, looking around as the chill settled in through her clothes. 'I've no idea what either of us is doing here.'

'Ah,' said Mr Princewell, taking another sip of coffee and setting his cup down again. 'Then I have a little explaining to do . . .'

About half an hour later, George staggered out of the dungeon staircase and into the light. Rupert, who had been hovering nearby, zoomed over to ask if she was all right, and if there was anything he could do to help.

'I just need to sit down for a moment,' George said palely, and, while she got her breath back, she refused to answer any of his other questions. Rupert continued his caring-uncle act until he saw he wasn't going to get anything out of her, so he slipped down the staircase to see to their guest, while George made her way back to the camp.

'You seem quiet,' Anne said as she sat down. 'Julian's been going on and on to the journalists all afternoon about how we should stay in Britain.'

*'Let's be completely honest about this, he said, smiling.
'Krexit means Krexit.'*

'Good for him,' said George.

'But, now it's nearly dinner time, everyone seems to be losing interest and calming down. By the way, you should have seen – after doing a few television interviews, the people at work spotted Julian and phoned to say it didn't look like he was working from home. They gave him a written warning, which got him in a temper.'

'Good for him,' said George.

'I was going to make us dinner over the fire, but you wouldn't believe what some of the food stalls are selling down on the beach – it's like a warm-up for Camp Bestival down there. Anyway, there's falafel wraps, sushi, all sorts. There are even some local bands playing.'

'So that's why I've got a headache,' said George. 'Why can't someone go down and tell all these horrible intruders that the only people who are allowed on the island are us, and the occasional smuggler or spy?'

Anne smiled. 'Yes,' she said. 'Or perhaps, once in a while, a small band of international jewel thieves? That would be far preferable to this lot. Those were the days.' She could tell that something was troubling George, and she knew that approaching the subject directly would be no use at all. 'Come on,' she said, 'let's go down to the beach; it's happy hour – we can get two-for-one caipirinhas.'

'There's a bar?'

'There are two. One of them's got a generator and is showing the first day of Wimbledon.'

'Oh, go on, then. That does sound nice,' said George, getting up.

Anne squeezed her shoulder and gave her a kiss.

The next morning, Julian woke up, aware that a noise had just roused him. In his befuddled state, he seemed to think that it had been the sound of his sister sleepily begging someone called Henrik not to return to Sweden, because she had 'never felt like this before' and was 'sure something could be worked out'.

Julian dismissed this ridiculous notion, but, unable to nod off again, he was left with his own thoughts. He found that his stomach was churning, his pulse was racing and that he had been left trembling and sweaty from whatever he had been dreaming about. It was just like he had felt after the cheese dream from the stolen Gorgonzola, except worse. He unzipped the sleeping bag to get cool air on his body and lay there, his heart gradually slowing to normal, as he tried to make his thoughts slow down too.

Three nights on the trot, he had woken with this same feeling of fresh panic and horror. What did it mean? Was he really starting to have misgivings about the sort of people he had made his political bedfellows? Was he beginning to suffer from that horrible word which had sprung to life just a few days before – Regrexit? What would he suffer from if he felt badly after the Kirrin Island referendum? *Kregrexit*? How many more bloody awful words was this ghastly mess going to throw up? Did the English language have to die along with Britain's ties to the European Union?

Lying there in the dark, he finally asked himself, truly and honestly, whether he would have voted the same way if he had thought for a moment that Britain might genuinely leave the EU. And he did not know the answer. Sometimes after a crucial event it could be maddeningly hard to recall what your mood had been beforehand, even when it was just days ago.

Gradually, as his thoughts slowed and he relaxed again, he saw a glow spread across the sky. He sat up so he could see it reflected on the water. And on the beach. No matter what, this would always be one of the most wonderful places on earth, he thought. And then he suddenly realized what he was looking at.

'George,' he said, kneeling over her. 'George, I think you ought to wake up. You'll want to see this . . .'

'What?' said George, turning over. She had also been woken by Anne's murmurings about the handsome Henrik, and was only just getting back to sleep. 'It can't be morning after orange,' she said. 'I haven't got my car alarm.'

'George, you're talking nonsense,' said Julian. 'Wake up; come with me. The beach is empty!'

George followed Julian down to the water's edge and stood, staring at the empty sand, shaking her head to wake herself up.

'It's some sort of miracle,' she said. 'My prayers have been answered.'

'It certainly seems most odd,' Julian said.

'Maybe we missed the Rapture, and the journalists were all called to heaven,' said George.

Julian guffawed, and George chuckled too.

'Back for another breakfast hotdog?' said a voice behind

What would he suffer from if he felt badly after the Kirrin Island referendum? **Kregrexit?**

them. They turned to see Bernie, all on his own, standing next to his hotdog stand.

'Breakfast of champions,' said George. 'Two please, Bernie.' She looked out over the beach – it was blessedly empty, except for one or two pieces of litter. But that was a small price to pay for freedom. She would happily collect the litter later in the day herself, while throwing sticks for Timmy.

'Can you tell us what's happened?' asked Julian.

'You're lucky my stall's still up – I was supposed to be gone by now meself,' Bernie said. 'My cousin's took his stuff off on the boat first, and promised to come back for me. You see, everyone started moving out in the middle of the night – once they heard about the other island.' He paused, looking awkward.

George and Julian looked at each other, perplexed.

'Other island?' Julian asked.

'You mean . . . Portland?' said George.

'*Portland*?' Bernie shuddered. 'Nah, they haven't gone to prison. So you haven't heard, then? Look, it seems there's another island nearby, don't ask me where, and that's where the next big story is. Word got around among the journos in the middle of the night, and, once they started moving out, everyone else followed toot sweet. The party's moved over there.'

'That suits me to a T,' said George, 'but, for God's sake, explain – *what* other island? You're local, you found this place – you must have an idea!'

'Listen,' Bernie said. 'I can only pass on what I overheard people telling each other as they were rushing to get away. Can't say I understood it, exactly. But . . .' He hesitated again, refusing to meet their eyes. Then he screwed up his courage to get it out. 'From what I heard, it seems it's that Rupert bloke – your press agent. It's all to do with him. You'd better just ask him, I reckon.'

'Well, that makes sense,' said Julian. 'If something shifty's going on, he has to be involved.'

'We will ask him,' George said. 'Thanks, Bernie.'

'I've got to admit, you're taking this better than I expected,' the hotdog man said.

'It's a blessing!' said George. 'The very last thing I wanted was all these people coming here. I mean, Julian will miss the attention, I suppose . . .'

Julian shrugged. 'I enjoyed it while it lasted. And maybe it was good practice for the future.'

'Oh, look, and there's Timmy. We must be near the

end of a chapter. May I have a last frankfurter, for my dog?'

'Have two.'

'You *are* nice. Here, Timmy! Breakfast! Sausages!'

'Woof!' barked Timmy, racing over. 'Woof, woof!'

CHAPTER ELEVEN

All is Explained

'It's a mystery wrapped in an enigma,' said Anne, as they ate breakfast around the fire. 'I wonder what can be going on?'

The Kirrin Castle camp was reduced to five once more. Half an hour ago, feeling that the crisis had passed and they had done their bit to soothe relations, Uncle Quentin and Aunt Fanny had set off on the row home. The island was back – almost – to how it had been before.

'There's no telling yet, because Rupert's not answering his phone,' said George.

'Leave a message?' said Dick.

'I've left three, but I daresay they will have little effect. Whatever he's up to, he clearly doesn't need us any longer.'

'Wait a minute,' said Anne. 'He's camped out with about half the British press right now. The half who aren't sitting outside 10 Downing Street, I mean. Why don't we just turn on the radio?'

Everyone murmured agreement at this solid good sense, and then endured George's furious swearing as she adjusted the aerial on the portable radio, until they could hear the *Today* programme with relative clarity.

'Julian, I'm getting you a bloody digital one of these for Christmas,' George muttered, sitting back.

Then they sat, sipping their coffee, and listened to sports, weather, governmental resignations, votes of no confidence and further dire news of the crashing value of sterling, before they heard what they had been waiting for.

'In surprising news this morning,' John Humphrys said in a cheerful voice, happy to move to a lighter story, 'a *second* breakaway state has been announced off the coast of Dorset. This comes after the declaration of the independence of Kirrin Island, last Friday. Even more surprising to some, the figurehead for this new small nation is the *cousin* of the current president of Kirrin Island, Georgina Kirrin.'

'It's GEORGE!' yelled George.

'We cross to him, now. For the second time in so many days, I get to say welcome, President Kirrin – and to a different person!'

Rupert's voice chuckled smoothly through the speakers, drawing gasps and groans from everyone there. 'Yes, it does seem to be a surprising turn up, doesn't it?' he said.

'Hiss!' said Anne. 'Hiss, boo!'

'You see, when my cousin declared independence, I was hoping to guide her through certain business deals that I knew would be hugely mutually beneficial for her and other parties, and create a large amount of business for the British Isles. Unfortunately, despite my best efforts, a satisfactory deal was never reached. But then I quickly realized that, with the land I inherited after my mother passed away, last year, I could perhaps pursue these advantages myself.'

'I understand that the land you live on is not technically an island at this time?' asked Humphrys.

'That is correct, John,' said Rupert, 'both "technically" and "at this time". But the land is on a narrow isthmus, you see, and, having hired the finest land-movers in the business on an achievement-related pay-scale, I hope to be able to confirm island status shortly after lunchtime tomorrow.'

'So you reckon this island's worth £350 million then?'
George asked.

'Amazing,' said Humphrys. 'Of course, "island status", as you put it, is not necessary to secure independence. But it seems as though it *is* necessary to your intentions . . .'

'Exactly correct,' Rupert agreed. 'You see, I am offering a one-stop solution for various multinational firms who have concerns over their tax liability. And to them I offer a very sympathetic ear.' His voice had become so smooth by this point, it was practically like treacle.

'You can almost hear how wealthy he's going to become, just from his voice!' said Dick.

'Double hiss!' said Anne. 'Double, triple boo and hiss!'

But Humphrys had not finished with Rupert. 'So, all that you just said is really just tricky talk for saying you're going to let multinationals base their companies on your island so they can dodge tax, in exchange for enormous fees to your good self.'

'All I will say,' said Rupert, gliding beneath the accusation with all the guilt and awkwardness of a limousine, 'is that this is going to generate a fantastic amount of direly needed investment into the local economy.'

'But, seeing as you're going to be living on a small island by tea time tomorrow, the "local economy" is essentially just you, isn't it?' asked John Humphrys.

Rupert paused. 'Well, there are some chickens in the back garden,' he said. 'But apart from them, yes.'

Dick switched the radio off with a curse.

'What a *rat*,' he said. 'What a rotter! What a . . . bloody *creep*!'

Julian and Anne chimed in with expressions of their disgust too. Next, it was George's turn. Everyone felt on tenterhooks, waiting for her reaction.

'I'm not so sure he hasn't done us a favour,' she said quietly.

'But George!' said Julian, aghast. 'He's robbed you of money. Lots of money. *Millions*, potentially!'

'He hasn't robbed me of anything,' said George. 'I'd already turned it down.'

She allowed their exclamations of astonishment to die down before continuing. 'It happened yesterday, and it's been weighing on me ever since.' She hesitated, scratching the dirt with a stick.

They all waited for her to go on, but she cleared her throat and looked away from them for a moment, then swallowed. 'This is the hardest thing I've ever had to say to you guys, and I hope you will be able to forgive me at the end. So. I'll just say it.'

'We know already, George!' wailed Anne.

'No, it's not *that*, Anne, you lovely, silly girl.' George laughed. Then she became serious again, and went on quickly: 'Yesterday, Rupert arranged a meeting between me and a representative from a very large multinational conglomerate. We met down in the castle dungeon, so no one would spot us speaking – although, he did almost all of the speaking, really. He offered me a large amount of money to make Kirrin Island the European HQ of his company. Whatever number you're thinking about – it was much larger than that. Just remember that purr in Rupert's voice a minute ago, and that will give you an idea.

'I asked for a chance to think about it. But, in the end, I only had to think about it for two seconds. And it broke my heart.'

'Well, of *course* it did!' said Julian.

'Not for the reason you're thinking. I couldn't care less about the money; I'd have given most of my share to charity, anyway. But I knew, if I accepted the money, I'd have to split it with the other original residents of Kirrin Island: you three. So I was turning it down on your behalf. *That's* the awful thing.' She paused and allowed them to ponder that for a few moments.

There was a heavy silence while they all thought about the money. And then, irresistibly, their thoughts moved to what they already had – the things that really mattered to them.

The silence was punctured by Dick blowing a raspberry. 'Easy come, easy go,' he said.

The others laughed. But then they all thought a few moments more about the money.

'So,' Anne said at length. 'Tell us why you had to say no.'

'There are some basic, practical things,' George said, glad to have the chance to explain. 'First, this island can't be an administrative capital, even of shell companies, without there being buildings on it. You need an address, after all. So they'd have to find somewhere to build, which would probably mean knocking most of the rest of the castle down, or digging up most of the two beaches, possibly even building a bridge to the mainland, and roads. All of which would be as horrible as it was fruitless. But that's not the real reason I said no.

'The real reason is that everyone, as far as I can see, throughout this whole referendum process, has been out to make personal profit from it. I made my announcement

There, squatting down, Timmy laid his profound expression of the democratic process.

from the heart, as a sincere rejection of all the values and attitudes that we've seen coming out in recent weeks. That's why people paid attention to us in the first place, and latched on to it as a story – because they detected that here was one small thing that was sincere. So, for me – or, rather, for all of us on Kirrin – to profit financially from it, would just be ... It would be the final and complete betrayal of values. It just couldn't be done. You do all see, don't you?'

'Of course we do, my darling,' said Anne. 'And I'm sorry you had to carry that on your shoulders, for even so much as a day.'

'Thank you, Anne,' said George, letting out a long sigh.

Everyone there suddenly felt very tired. This adventure on Kirrin Island hadn't panned out how they had hoped at all. It felt like the best thing for them now was to go home again, and try to pretend that it had never happened.

'I say,' said Dick. 'If any of those journalists ever catches up with us and asks us what the result of our referendum was, what shall we tell them?'

'Hmm,' said George. 'Well, why don't we hold it now and get it over with?'

'Suits me,' said Julian, standing up. 'As acting returning officer for the electoral roll of Kirrin Isla—'

'Oh, do shut up, Julian,' said Anne. 'Let's just do the vote.'

'Fair enough,' he said. 'I vote "In", George votes "Out". So, how do you two vote?'

The two campaign leaders watched Anne and Dick, and waited.

'We've discussed this,' said Dick, looking to Anne for encouragement. 'After all the division caused by Britain's referendum, we don't want Kirrin's referendum to throw up the possibility of further division among us.'

'It's too ghastly to contemplate,' said Anne. 'So, for the good of the group, and the country, I abstain.' She bowed her head, thinking of handsome Dieter, and wondering whether he would ever get round to asking her out, no matter what the political situation.

'By God, Dick!' said Julian. 'That throws the whole decision into your hands!'

'I, too, abstain,' said Dick. 'Is that grammatical? I, as well, also, do.'

Julian and George thought about that for a second, and then looked at each other. A moment passed, and they smiled.

'So you reckon this island's worth £350 million, then?' George asked.

'Ah, now . . . I should say, that was taken entirely out of context. That estimate was based on the best facts available to me at the time, and, in the cold light of day . . .'

'Disgraceful,' said George.

'Also, George, if you don't mind, I've an announcement,' said Anne.

George wondered if it was perhaps about one of the dishy exotic men she kept talking about in her sleep, but it soon appeared not.

'I have been greatly honoured to serve in the position of Home Secretary to Kirrin Island – and I shall never forget it. But I feel that I have done what I set out to do in the role, and therefore it's time for me to embark on new challenges. And so I hereby resign.'

'Oh, yes,' said Dick. 'I've also been honoured, and all that. But I also resign.'

'If Anne jumped off a cliff, would you do that as well?' asked George.

'Of *course*,' he said. 'There might be a chance of saving her!'

Anne smiled, and kissed him on the shoulder.

'I feel I must resign my position as well,' said Julian. 'After the flotilla fight, I feel my position has become untenable and I would like to resign to allow for a smooth transition.'

'Blimey,' said George, as they all sat next to her around the remains of the fire, and Dick started raking out the ashes with a long stick. 'A clean sweep. Well, having taken stock of your decisions, and in response to this vote of no confidence, I firmly vow to cling on to power for the rest of my days. So stick that in your pipe.'

Just then, Timmy came running past and, seeing them, stopped. They all looked at him.

'Timmy!' George said.

'Woof!' said the dog.

'I forgot about you – you have the deciding vote in the referendum. How do you vote, my dearest, darling boy?'

Timmy felt shy. He was already feeling the effects of the hotdogs. Tucking his tale between his legs, he retreated across the camp, past the campfire and the tents, past the nearly empty whiskey bottle and the cricket bat, to a bush twenty feet away. There, squatting down, he laid his profound expression of the democratic process.

'Timmy!' said George. 'That's disgusting!'

'Well said, Timmy!' called Anne. 'Well said!'

'Hear, hear!' said Dick.

'Woof,' said Timmy, dejectedly.

'I feel that I have done what I set out to do in the role and therefore it's time for me to embark on new challenges. And so I hereby resign.'